An I Can Read Book®

THE FAT CAT SAT ON THE MAT

S0-ADN-702

written and illustrated by

NURIT KARLIN

Scholastic Inc.

New York   Toronto   London   Auckland   Sydney

ISBN 0-590-14861-3

12 11 10 9 8 7 6 5 4 3 2 1   7 8 9/9 0 1 2/0

Printed in the U.S.A.   23
First Scholastic printing, September 1997

To Shira and Zohar

Wilma the witch has a crazy broom.

It likes to fly around her room.

She also has a fat cat

and a pet rat.

6

Wilma loves her pet rat.

She calls the rat

"my little brat."

The rat hates the cat.

The cat does not care.

The cat, who is fat,

just lies in the vat

and stares at the rat.

The rat hates that.

One night, when Wilma was out,

the fat cat got out of the vat.

He went, *pit-a-pat*,

and sat on the mat.

9

"This is MY mat!" said the rat.

"So what," said the cat.

"So get off!" said the rat.

"No I won't," said the cat.

"Then I will go and get my bat,"
said the rat.

"It will get you off the mat."

"No it won't," said the cat.

"This is the mat of the rat,"
said the bat.

"So what," said the cat.

"So get off!" said the bat.

"No I won't," said the cat.

"Then I will go and get my hat,"
said the bat.

"It will get you off the mat."

"No it won't," said the cat.

"This is the mat of the rat,"
said the hat.

"So what," said the cat.

"So get off!" said the hat.

"No I won't," said the cat.

"I am a cat, and I am fat.

No rat, no bat, no hat

can move me.

I shall sit on this mat

for as long as I wish."

"We shall see," said the hat.

"Look what we have," said the hat.

"Big deal, a dish," said the cat.

"A dish and what else?" asked the hat.

"Mmmm . . . a fish!" said the cat.

"A fish on a dish," said the hat.

"For me?" asked the cat.

"Yes, for you," said the hat.

"Bring it closer," said the cat.

"Come and get it," said the hat.

17

"You think I am stupid,"

said the cat.

"You want to get me off the mat.

I won't get off, and that is that!"

Rat-a-tat . . .

"What was that?" asked the bat.

"I don't know," said the hat.

Rat-a-tat . . .

"It sounds like a rat with a tat,"
said the cat.

"It is not me," said the rat.

"What is a tat?" asked the bat.

"I don't know," said the hat.

"Look! The broom!" cried the bat.

The broom flew into the room.

It zoomed over the mat,

over the cat,

over the hat and the bat

and Wilma's pet rat.

The fish flew off the dish.

It landed on the hat,

which landed on the bat,

who landed on the rat,

who landed on the cat,

lying flat on the mat.

24

"Get off!" said the cat.

"No we won't!" said the hat

and the bat and the rat.

The fish said nothing.

Wilma came home.

She looked at the room.

She picked up the broom.

Then she asked,

"Why is the fish out of the dish?"

"Because of the cat," said the rat.

"The fat cat sat on my mat!"

"My dear little brat," said Wilma,

"what makes you think

this is YOUR mat?"

The fat cat smiled.

The fat cat got up

and stretched.

Off flew the rat, the bat,

and the hat.

He ate the fish,

   licked the dish,

      and went back

         to lie down in the vat.

"Thank goodness!"

said the mat.